Follow the Leader

by Miriam Sklar

ISBN: 978-1-338-75075-1
Illustrated by John Lund

Published by Scholastic Inc., 557 Broadway, New York, NY 10012

10 9 8 7 6 5 4 68 25 26 27/0

Printed in Jiaxing, China. First printing, January 2021.

Let us run!

Let us jump!

Let us march!

Let us skip!

Let us spin!

Let us hop!

Let us stop!